Dear Grandma,
How are y[ou]
You wo[uld] travels? what
Barry did! He ate
a metal spoon! We
saw the X-ray. It
looked like this

← poor Barry
and guess over
what happened
Next?

Dear Tessa, you up xo
what are days? I miss
these a lot. what is
you r New school like?
r there: I am ha-
Mr. D's
we are and

Copyright © 2021 by Zoey Abbott

Tundra Books, an imprint of Penguin Random House Canada Young Readers, a division of Penguin Random House of Canada Limited

All rights reserved. The use of any part of this publication reproduced, transmitted in any form or by any means, electronic, mechanical, photocopying, recording, or otherwise, or stored in a retrieval system, without the prior written consent of the publisher — or, in case of photocopying or other reprographic copying, a licence from the Canadian Copyright Licensing Agency — is an infringement of the copyright law.

LIBRARY AND ARCHIVES CANADA CATALOGUING IN PUBLICATION

Title: I do not like Yolanda / Zoey Abbott.
Names: Abbott, Zoey, author, illustrator.
Identifiers: Canadiana (print) 20190187174 | Canadiana (ebook) 20190187182 |
ISBN 9780735266513 (hardcover) | ISBN 9780735266520 (EPUB)
Classification: LCC PZ7.1.A23 Ia 2021 | DDC j813/.6—dc23

Published simultaneously in the United States of America by Tundra Books of Northern New York,
an imprint of Penguin Random House Canada Young Readers, a division of Penguin Random House of Canada Limited

Library of Congress Control Number: 2019949972

Edited by Samantha Swenson
Designed by Five Seventeen and Kate Sinclair
The artwork in this book was rendered in ink, gouache and colored pencil.
The text was set in Carre Noir Pro.

Printed and bound in China

www.penguinrandomhouse.ca

1   2   3   4   5   25   24   23   22   21

Penguin
Random House
tundra TUNDRA BOOKS

For the real Bianca and the real Yolanda (who used to work at the Noe Valley Post Office and once recreated Babette's feast)

Special thanks to Olive Wagner for the whittled stick-pens used in this book

Abbott, Zoey,
I do not like Yolanda /
[2021]
33305251609842
sa   05/28/21

I Do Not Like Yolanda

Zoey Abbott

tundra

I LOVE writing letters.

I LOVE stamps.

And I do NOT like Yolanda.

Stamps are beautiful and I collect them, actually.

I snip them off the letters I get. My grandpa gave me a box of his old stamps too.

They are cream colored with
beautiful dark ink and portraits of
queens, villains and exotic birds.

Here's who I write letters to:

My pen pal in Sri Lanka

My grandma in Washington, D.C.

My other grandma who travels on a boat around the world

My uncle Kenta

And my friend who moved to Uganda

Here's who I do NOT write letters to:

Yolanda

Writing letters is HARD work.

You've got to think ahead and spell things correctly
so that someone else can read them.

You've got to have interesting things to say,
otherwise you might just bore their pants off.

The post office is no big deal.

What I'm really afraid of is getting in Yolanda's line.

That lady gives me nightmares.

I don't think Yolanda likes kids very much.

Or adults for that matter . . .

One time, I spent an hour on my envelope drawings.

My letter was a little bit heavy, so Yolanda weighed it . . .

. . . and this happened!

Another time, her scaly talons
reached out for my coins . . .

and I flinched.

(Seriously, who wouldn't?!)

Well, that day I didn't even get to send my letter because I came up five cents short.

If you are standing in line and there are three postal windows open, you've got a one-in-three chance you're going to get Yolanda.

(I always cross EVERYTHING for good luck.)

I think she'd like to eat me up one day. She has probably eaten up dozens of people by now.

But today, I'm too excited to be afraid because I've written five letters, and three of them have drawings too — on the inside, of course.

I'll need three domestic and two international stamps because my one grandma just docked in New Zealand.

Today, I'm not going to be afraid of Yolanda. And if she tries to eat me up, I'll eat her up right back.

So, I gather all my lucky charms.

I do all my
luckiest things.

And I cross my everythings. I will NOT
let Yolanda ruin my Five Letter Day.

I get to the post office, and
there's only one window open.
And it's guess who.

I think to myself . . . I am NOT going
to run (even though I want to!).

I clutch my letters tight . . . .

And I start walking toward Yolanda.

All of a sudden, I'm in front of her.

She looks pretty hungry, but I lift my chin and say in
my most assured voice,

"I'll take three domestics and two internationals,
please, and how was your weekend?"

Yolanda's mouth starts to open, and it occurs to me
that I've never technically seen her teeth before, but
I'm about to . . .

And I think, great, this is what I get for having a
Five Letter Day.

Yolanda's eyes narrow and she leans forward,
coming in for the kill.

I close my eyes and think *this is it*.

"Well, I just served one of the most delightful meals
that anyone has ever prepared."

I open one eye and see that her teeth are not as pointy as I had expected. She doesn't have her talons out.

And she's smiling at me!

So I lean in and say, "That sounds cool.
Tell me more!"

She explains it and it DOES sound delightful . . .

She prepared a seven-course meal described in
her favorite book, *Babette's Feast*.

She tells me about turtle soup, buckwheat
pancakes with caviar, sour cream and rum sponge
cake with figs, candied cherries, cheeses and
fruits.

I'm starting to feel hungry.

NEXT WI
please

Then, all of a sudden, I have my five letters and five stamps in one hand and my change in the other.

And I am wondering, what is caviar? And what does Yolanda's kitchen look like?

But since I write a lot of letters, I know I will be back at the post office in a couple of days.

I'll try to get in Yolanda's line, so I can ask her.

Dear **Yolanda,**

How are you? I'm fine. Yesterday my dad and I made the most delicious Lentil Soup! It's my great grandmother Laurene's recipe. I think you would like it.

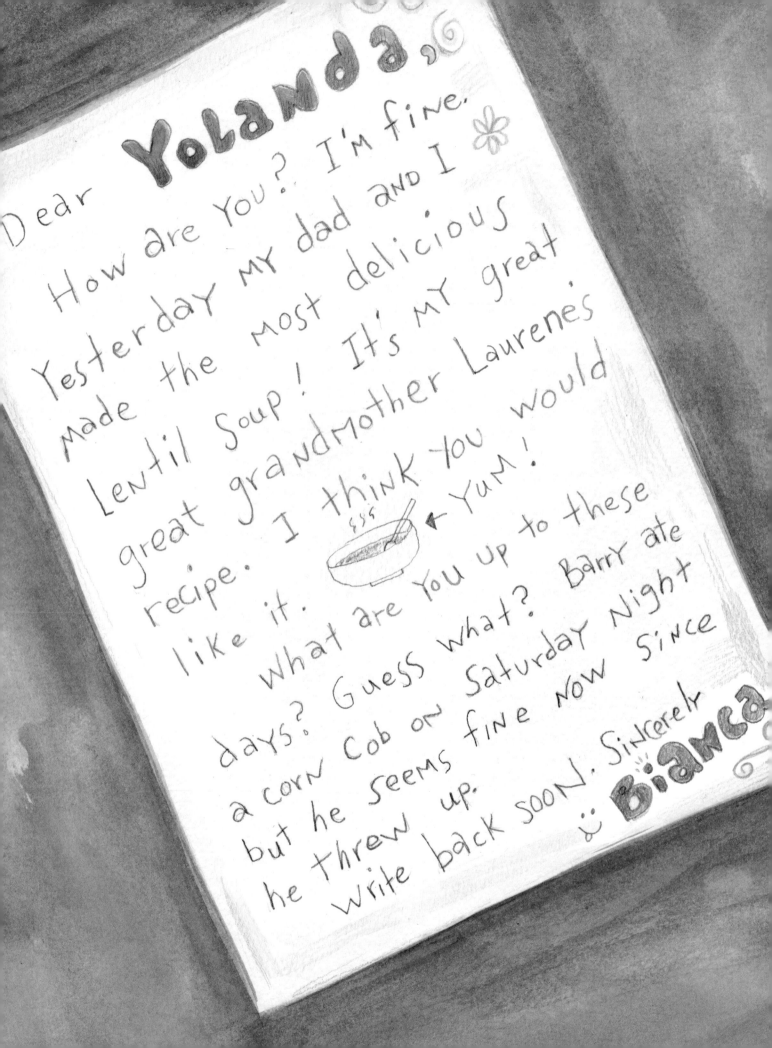
sss ← Yum!

What are you up to these days? Guess what? Barry ate a corn cob on Saturday Night but he threw up. he seems fine now Since write back soon. Sincerely, **Bianca**